TOWN AND COUNTRY PUBLIC LIBRARY
3 2990 00102 11
WITHDRAW

D0852668

MY BROTHER IS A ROBOT

BOOK 6

THE DECISION

AMANDA RONAN

The Decision
My Brother is a Robot #6

Published by Scobre Educational

Written by Amanda Ronan

Printed in the United States of America.

Scobre Educational
2255 Calle Clara
La Jolla, CA 92037

Scobre Operations & Administration
42982 Osgood Road
Fremont, CA 94539

www.scobre.com
info@scobre.com

Scobre Educational publications may be purchased for educational, business, or sales promotional use.

Cover and layout design by Nicole Ramsay
Copyedited by Kristin Russo

ISBN: 978-1-62920-510-6 (Library Bound)
ISBN: 978-1-62920-509-0 (eBook)

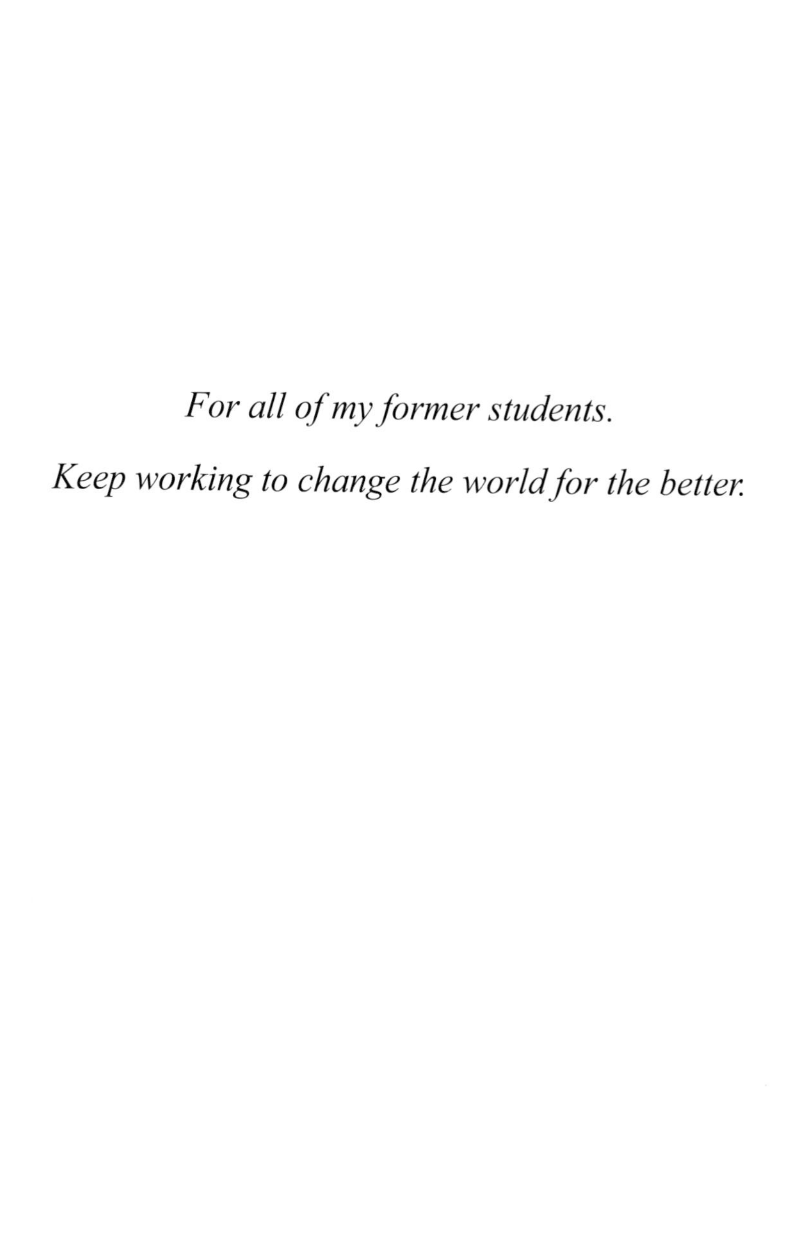

For all of my former students.

Keep working to change the world for the better.

CHAPTER 1

I SAT AT THE KITCHEN TABLE AND WATCHED MY DAD FLIP SOME mushrooms in the frying pan. He was preparing a gourmet meal as a homecoming for my brother Cyrus.

I reached under the table and patted our basset hound, Scooter, on the head. Looking up at my dad I asked, “Why are worrying about making such a fancy dinner? It’s not like Cyrus can eat it.”

Cyrus was my twin brother, but he was actually a robot. My mom, who was an engineer, developed the most lifelike robot ever and made him look just like me. Last year, she brought him home so he could learn human emotions and study human behavior up close. Things with Cyrus were a little rocky at first. I didn't know how to handle having a brother, especially one who was super smart and nearly perfect. I took advantage of the situation and had Cyrus do my homework for me, which got me kicked off the basketball team. That made my Dad angry. Dad didn't like the idea of a robot living in the house like a human and he wanted my mom to take Cyrus back to the lab.

Cyrus was smart, though, and he found out all sorts of interesting facts about my dad, including that he loved to cook. So, to get on his good side, Cyrus planned to remodel the kitchen for my dad. Of course, that didn't quite work out as planned. Cyrus ended up tearing the house apart, and Dad had to help him rebuild it. During their work on the renovation, though, Cyrus and Dad bonded, and we became a close family.

Cyrus was always trying to help me out. Once, after I'd finally gotten back on the basketball team, I had to miss a game. Cyrus offered to play in my place. When one of Mom's jealous colleagues at the lab found out that we'd switched places, he made the whole town worried that robots would try to take over human lives. The story made people nervous and the lab nearly shut down Mom and Cyrus's program. To help, my friends and I launched a social media campaign to show the world how great Cyrus is. A video of Cyrus helping a boy who was stuck in a skee-ball machine went viral and the lab agreed to let Cyrus stay with us. After that, Mom and Dad adopted him and we became a real family.

But life didn't calm down too much after that, either. When Cyrus and I started middle school this year, I got jealous of his popularity. All the older kids wanted to hang out with him and he started making new friends. On top of it all, I didn't make the basketball team. I got really angry and picked a fight with him in the hallway. We were able to settle our differences with the help of the school guidance counselor.

But then, seven months ago our family life changed completely. A hurricane hit our town and we had to collect supplies and take cover. The experience made Cyrus curious about human survival, so Dad took him on a survival camping trip. When they got back, Cyrus shut himself in the work shed and started building something. He finally shared his invention with us. It was a machine that could create drinkable water from dirt, rocks, and soil. He named it the 3SNC, for Shawn, Samira, Scooter, Nathaniel, and Cyrus. Since his discovery, Cyrus has been traveling all over the world sharing his machine and working with other scientists on new projects.

"Just because he can't eat the food, doesn't mean he won't appreciate it. Aren't you excited to see your brother?" Dad asked, dipping a spoon into the sauce boiling on the stovetop.

Scooter's ears perked up, hoping he might get a taste, too.

I shrugged. "I guess. I barely remember what it's like to have a brother. I went through the whole sixth grade without him," I said sarcastically. I mean, I really *had* missed Cyrus, a lot. But I had to be cool.

"Why don't you go work on your homework so that you guys can spend some time together after dinner?" Dad nodded to my backpack hanging off my chair.

"You mean I have to go to school tomorrow? This isn't like a national holiday or something?" I asked because my parents had been treating it like one. All they could talk about was Cyrus's homecoming.

My dad looked at me over his shoulder, but he didn't have to say a thing, his glare said it all.

"Okay, okay. Come on, Scoot, let's go get to work," I said, heaving my bag over one shoulder. I worked on my homework for about an hour until I heard Mom's car pull into the driveway.

"So what was Kenya like?" I asked, shoving a piece of garlic bread in my mouth.

Cyrus shrugged. "Hot and dry."

"But wasn't it awesome? Did you go on safari? Did you see lions?" My brother sat across from me at the table, and even though we were twins, he looked like he was about ten years older than when he'd left.

"Shawn." My mom smiled at me. "Why don't you eat this delicious dinner, and Cyrus will tell you all about his travels later? He looks tired."

Cyrus nodded. "I am, actually. I'm going to go upload my travel files for the day and shut down my systems for the night. Can I use your office?" he asked Mom.

"You can sleep in my room!" I offered, wanting to

spend as much time with him as possible. Cyrus was only home for a week and I wanted to make the most of it.

Cyrus shook his head. "No, I don't want to bother you while I reboot. The traveling has made some of my circuitry a little noisy. I sound like an unoiled Tin Man."

"Uh-oh, we'll take a look tomorrow, okay?" Mom asked, putting her hand over Cyrus's. "Will you run a diagnostic report and email it to me so I can see what needs to get done?"

Cyrus nodded and stood up. He stopped behind my dad and hugged him. "The dinner looked great. I can see you used the aged cheddar. Nice choice."

My dad shot me an "I told you so" look and then turned to Cyrus and said, "Goodnight, son. Sleep well."

I watched as Cyrus walked out of the room and then turned back to my parents. "I thought we were going to get to hang out tonight?"

My mom frowned, “I know. I’m sorry, Shawn. Your brother is really tired. His system is stressed out from all the travel. He’ll be as good as new tomorrow. Just wait and see.”

CHAPTER 2

THE NEXT MORNING, I GOT OUT OF BED AS SOON AS MY alarm went off. Normally I'd hit snooze a few times, but that morning I got up early to see Cyrus. I was hoping we could play a few levels of our favorite video game, Total Pizza Calamity, before I had to go to school.

I raced down the stairs and into the kitchen. Dad was sitting at the table drinking coffee and eating a bagel.

"Where's Cyrus?" I asked pointing at his empty space at the table.

"At the lab. He and your mom left about an hour ago," Dad said, turning the page of the newspaper he was reading. You'd think my dad would have embraced the technology age with his engineer wife and robot son, but my dad would not give up his newspaper. He refused to read the news online like a normal person.

"Why didn't anyone wake me?" I complained.

"You wanted us to wake you at five thirty? Normally you like to get more beauty sleep than that," Dad said, grinning.

"Yeah, well, I thought I'd get to see Cyrus. He's not working this whole trip, is he?" I asked, smearing my own bagel with grape jelly. I made sure Dad wasn't watching and let a little jelly fall to the floor for Scooter.

Not turning around, my dad announced, "I saw

that. Please don't feed the dog jelly and please don't get jelly on my kitchen floors. And no, I think they just went to the lab to fix Cyrus up after all the wear and tear."

I sighed and sat down with my dad at the table. "Do you think Cyrus is going to come back to school next year? All this attention about the 3SNC has to die down soon, right?"

My dad put down his newspaper, took off his glasses, and stuck them in his shirt pocket. "I'm not sure, Shawn. I think your brother has a lot going on right now and middle school is probably not at the top of the list of things to worry about."

I looked out the kitchen window. In the back yard was the shed where Cyrus has built his famous machine. "I understand. Cyrus never was like the other kids, you know, being a robot and all. I just thought he might want his old life back. But, I guess, what he's doing is more important now, you know, for the whole world."

My dad stared at me, studying my face for a time. "Do you mean that or are you saying it sarcastically?"

I shook my head. "No, I mean it. Cyrus made something amazing and he has a duty to share it."

"That's very mature of you, son. The old Shawn would have been jealous at the attention Cyrus was getting," Dad said.

I snickered, "Um, jealous of all that boring science talk all day? Not this guy," I laughed, trying to play off the compliment from my dad.

He smiled. "Look, I know you want to see Cyrus and I know he wants to see you, too. Why don't we all go out and see a movie tonight?"

"Really?" I asked. "But it's a school night."

My dad laughed, "As long as you finish your homework first. Now, finish up your breakfast and get ready for school."

I shoved the rest of my bagel in my mouth and grabbed the entertainment section from Dad's newspaper. "Come on, Scooter. Let's go pick out a movie to watch tonight. Do you think Cyrus wants to watch a lovey-dovey, romantic comedy?" I laughed as Scooter tilted his head to one side. "No? How about an action movie? I think *Rising Storm* is playing." Scooter howled his approval and then rolled over for a belly rub.

When I got to school, I was surprised to find a crowd of kids around my locker. When people saw me coming they started calling my name and asking me a million questions at once:

"Shawn, is Cyrus coming to school today?"

"Shawn, how's Cyrus?"

"Shawn, did Cyrus really meet the Queen of England?"

"Shawn, where's Cyrus?"

My best friend, James, pushed his way through the crowd shouting, "Okay people, move along! There's nothing to see here."

I felt relived as a few people walked away. They were still talking about when Cyrus was going to get to school, but at least they gave me some breathing room.

"What was that all about?" I asked James as I dropped off some books in my locker.

"You're the brother of the most famous robot in the world! Didn't you see the paparazzi waiting outside when the bus pulled in?" James asked nodding to the window.

I walked over and leaned my face against the glass. James wasn't kidding. There were two black SUVs near the school driveway. Inside the trucks were people holding cameras. "But Cyrus isn't even at school today."

We turned around and headed for our first class.

James said, “But they don’t know that. They want to get a shot of the famous robot and his human brother. It’s a story everyone’s interested in.”

“But they have the family photo we took in fifth grade,” I said mentioning the embarrassing Thanksgiving photo my parents had insisted we take. When Cyrus and his invention made the news, the media liked to show that photo as they talked about Cyrus’s background and family life.

James shrugged. “I guess they want something new. Where is Cy, anyway?”

“He’s at the lab getting fixed up. He was really tired and run down when he got home last night. We’re going out tonight, but maybe you can come over tomorrow. I’m sure he wants to see you,” I said as we walked through the door to our science class.

“Oh, I’m sure we’ll stop by. My mom has been talking about Cyrus’s homecoming for weeks. She’ll probably drop by with a plate of cookies and pretend like she forgot he was back," James laughed. Like many of the parents in town, James's mother loved the idea of having a robot kid.

As I sat down at the lab table and got out my homework, I felt a hand on my shoulder. I looked up to see Chantal. I had been in love with Chantal since third grade, but she had a crush on Cyrus.

"How is he?" Chantal whispered, sounding concerned.

"He's good. Fine," I answered. I could tell James the truth, but I didn't know how much I could trust Chantal. She was really popular and would probably tell everyone what I told her. There was enough gossip going around about Cyrus, I didn't want to add to it.

"Good," Chantal smiled. "Tell him I said 'hi.' Tell him to call me, okay?"

"Sure," I said, turning in my seat when our teacher Mr. Denny clapped his hands to start class. I tried to concentrate on my classes for the rest of the day, but it was tough. I wanted to be with Cyrus, laughing about all the attention he was getting, playing video games, and hanging out. I couldn't wait to go to the movies that night!

CHAPTER 3

"OKAY, I'M DONE WITH MY HOMEWORK," I ANNOUNCED AS I walked down the stairs into the living room.

My dad tossed his phone on the coffee table and sighed, "That was your mother. She said they won't be home for another few hours. I don't think we're going to the movies tonight, Shawn."

I sighed and turned to go back upstairs. "Oh."

Once I got to my room, I curled up on my bed and took a nap. I'd been looking forward to seeing Cyrus for weeks. The anticipation was exhausting. I didn't sleep very well, though. I kept having dreams about fighting with my brother. We were arguing about everything. I tossed and turned for an hour and then decided to get out of bed and go outside.

"Your mom just called again," Dad said. "I told her you were disappointed about not seeing your brother, so she invited us to come have dinner with them at the lab."

"Really?" I asked, grabbing my jacket from the hook by the door. "In the cafeteria?" Normally cafeteria food was nothing to get excited about. At school, the cafeteria food was mushy, beige, and unidentifiable. But at Smith and Company, the lab where my mom worked, the cafeteria was more like a gourmet buffet. They had king crab legs, all-you-can-eat pizza, and a sushi bar. It was awesome!

As Dad pulled onto the street where the lab was, he turned to me in the backseat and said, "I can see photographers camped out by the parking lot. Just try to ignore them, okay?"

I nodded and pressed my face to the glass to see the crowd. The security guard waved Dad through and quickly shut the gate behind our car to keep the paparazzi out. "I can't believe they're all here for Cyrus," I said to Dad as he pulled into the parking garage and out of sight of the cameras.

"Your brother is kind of a big deal right now. It might be like this for a while," Dad said as we rode the elevator to the twelfth floor.

"The last time I was here your office was the size of a broom closet. I guess having a robot son has really helped your cred around here," I joked as I walked into Mom's new office. Mom sat behind a huge oak desk and Cyrus was sitting on one of the two leather couches with a laptop on his knees.

Mom looked up from her work and smiled at me. "It's been a while since you've been here. They've expanded the research and development wings quite a bit and I got a cushy new office."

I looked at the paintings on the wall, some of which I recognized. "Is this my kindergarten finger painting?" I asked pointing to one.

Cyrus snickered, "No Shawn, that's a Jackson Pollock."

"A what?" I looked closer at the painting.

"Jackson Pollock. He's a famous abstract painter. You know, like a world-renowned artist," Cyrus said, standing up.

I shrugged. "Looks like splotches of paint. I'm pretty sure I made the same picture when I was five."

Cyrus sighed and wrapped his arm around my shoulder, "Oh, brother, you have so much to learn."

I laughed, "Like what?"

"Don't get me started," Cyrus grinned and I knew if I'd kept asking him, he would have started rattling off all kinds of useless information in his usual know-it-all brother robot kind of way. I smiled, thinking I finally had the old Cyrus back.

"Boys, I have to finish up this report. Cyrus, why don't you show Shawn around while I get some work done." She looked at her watch. "Meet your dad and me in the cafeteria in about forty-five minutes. Okay?"

We both nodded and started toward the door.

"Don't get into any trouble," Dad called after us, always trying to ruin the fun.

Cyrus nodded toward a double glass door at the end of the hallway and said, "Come on. Let's go get scooters!"

I jogged after him and watched as he punched a code into the number pad. The doors slid open to reveal a row of stand-up electric scooters. We each grabbed one. Cyrus rode his out of the room easily. It took me a few tries to figure out how to keep moving forward, but once I did, Cyrus and I were racing down the maze of hallways in the lab. We had to dodge a lot of the scientists, since most of them were still working in the building.

"Want to see some of the new projects the lab is working on? Top secret stuff?" Cyrus asked after we'd covered most of the floors a few times. He pointed to the end of the hallway. Two large metal doors sat locked and closed with a sign that said No Unauthorized Personnel in bright red letters.

As an unauthorized person, I should have said no. And after promising my dad to not get in trouble, I should have again said no. But I didn't. I grinned and nodded. "Totally."

Cyrus entered his code, had his eyeballs and fingerprints scanned, and rushed me through the doors when they opened. "Let's go over here, first. You have to see what they're doing with solar power."

CHAPTER 4

THE EVENING AT THE LAB HAD BEEN THE MOST FUN I'D HAD IN a long time. Cyrus showed me some amazing prototypes. Of course, I can't tell you too much about them—they're top secret. But trust me when I tell you that personal jetpacks are coming at you in the near future.

After dinner, Mom pulled Cyrus aside and had a private conversation with him. It looked like they were arguing, but I couldn't tell from where I was standing. When it was time to go home, Cyrus came with Dad and me, while Mom said she had to work a little while longer. She kissed my forehead and said goodnight. She promised we'd spend time together as a family over the weekend.

"What was that all about?" I whispered to Cyrus on the drive home.

"What was what all about?" Cyrus asked.

"Were you arguing with Mom?" I asked.

"No." Cyrus shrugged and looked out the window. I opened my mouth to keep prying, but he turned and said, "I think I'm going to come to school with you tomorrow. You know, to see everyone."

I smiled. "Really? That would be great. Everyone's asking about you!" I nudged his shoulder. "Even Chantal."

"She's been emailing me while I've been away," Cyrus admitted.

"Ah-ha! I knew there was something going on.

You said you didn't like her because you knew *I* did," I accused.

"I don't like her like that. Besides, she lives here and I live . . . I don't know where," Cyrus sighed.

"Um, you live here, too. Why would you say that?" I asked.

Cyrus turned and looked me right in the eyes. For the first time I saw that they looked different. I had brown eyes and so did Cyrus. Or at least he used to. But now, the eyes that were staring at me, full of sadness, were blue. "I didn't mean it. Of course I live here," Cyrus said as Dad turned the car into our driveway.

"Cyrus?" I said as my brother stepped out of the car. But he didn't hear me.

The noise in the cafeteria stopped as soon as we walked in. Everyone turned to look at Cyrus. Then the whispering started. Cyrus smiled casually. This kind of attention was nothing new for him. As he started walking toward our usual table in the middle of the lunchroom, some of the lunch monitors began to clap. Then everyone joined in. Kids whistled and hollered.

Demarcus, one of the guys from my old basketball team, nodded at Cyrus and asked, "How do you deal with this all the time?"

Cyrus just shrugged and said, "I've gotten used to it. I guess I just focus on the fact that I want to help people."

"I think it's been cool to see you on all those talk shows and on the covers of those magazines. You're totally famous!" James exclaimed while eating his second turkey sandwich.

"All the press is tough," Cyrus said. "It takes time away from working with other scientists, which is what I really want to be doing."

"Where's the best place you've been?" Colton asked.

Cyrus thought about the question for a second. “Here . . . it’s good to be home.”

James laughed and said sarcastically, “Awww, that’s so sweet.”

Cyrus grinned. “You try traveling to twenty-five different countries, all with different languages, different customs, and different levels of scientific knowledge. All while part of your system sends and receives constant phone calls, emails, and texts. Not to mention the bad Wi-Fi connections in some places. Just trying to make life better for humans. Once you try all that . . . then you can tease me.”

Everyone looked around at each other. We didn’t know what to say. Cyrus’s new life seemed so glamorous, but he was definitely under some stress. I felt really bad that I hadn’t asked him about it before.

Cyrus could tell he’d made us uncomfortable, so he smiled and tried to laugh it off. “It’s just good to be home, you know?”

The guys all sighed, relieved they hadn't made Cyrus angry. But I could tell he was frustrated.

"I'm going to go say 'hi' to the guys on the soccer team," Cyrus said, standing up. "Shawn, Mom is picking me up in a few minutes, so I'll see you at home."

"You're leaving already?" I asked, looking up at the clock.

Cyrus nodded."Yeah. I need to go to the lab. There are a few things I need to take care of today." He walked out of the cafeteria to find his old friends.

"Remember when Cyrus would use his sensors to tell when you were stressed or angry?" James asked from across the table.

I nodded. "Yeah. He was always telling me to regulate my emotions."

"Well," James said, stealing a baby carrot from my barely-eaten lunch in front of me, "someone needs to remind Cyrus to regulate his own emotions. Dude is getting a little intense."

James was right. Cyrus needed a break before he had a breakdown.

CHAPTER 5

Mom and Cyrus were at the lab all night and still hadn't come home when I woke up. Dad didn't know when they'd be home, but he kept promising me we'd spend the weekend together doing normal family things. I had trouble believing it, since we hadn't done anything like a normal family in a long time.

At lunch, the guys all asked about Cyrus and wondered if he'd come back to school to visit again before he left on another trip. I could only shrug and tell them the truth, that I had no idea.

When the lunch bell rang I picked up my garbage and started for the door.

"Hey, Shawn!" I heard and looked over my shoulder to see Chantal waving at me.

"Hey," I smiled back. "Did you get to see Cyrus at all yesterday?"

"Yeah." She tucked her wavy brown hair behind her ear. "Actually, I wanted to tell you that Cyrus just texted me. He wanted me to tell you to meet him at Garner Park after school.

"He did? Why'd he tell you that and not me?" I reached for my phone and realized I'd left it in my backpack. The battery had died on the way to school, so I left it in my locker.

Chantal shrugged. "He couldn't get ahold of you and it seemed important, so he wanted me to give you the message. Tell him I said 'hi,' okay?"

I nodded. "Thanks, Chantal. I will."

Later that afternoon I got off the bus two stops earlier than usual and walked down the block to the park. There were a few little kids playing on the swings and a guy playing basketball, but Cyrus was nowhere to be seen. I couldn't text him because my phone was still dead, so I dropped my backpack to the ground and sat at the picnic bench to wait.

After just a few minutes of looking over my shoulder, waiting for Cyrus to appear, the guy playing basketball walked over.

"Hey," he said and sat across from me.

I was annoyed that he just sat down with even asking, so I gave him just a quick nod and went back to looking for Cyrus.

"You waiting for someone?" he asked, placing the basketball on the picnic table.

"Yeah, my brother," I said looking back at him. He was in his early twenties and had dark hair and blue eyes. He looked familiar, but I couldn't quite place where I'd seen him before.

The guy nodded and asked, "Your incredibly smart, handsome, and basically perfect brother?"

I looked closer at him. "Cyrus?"

He nodded and smiled. "Ta-da! What do you think?"

I shook my head, confused by what was happening. "I don't understand. I can't—I mean—I don't . . . "

"Mom and I worked all night to get the changes in place. It was time for me to grow up on the outside. It's been hard enough for people to accept that a robot can be a scientist, but when I showed up at labs and looked like a twelve-year-old, well, let's just say it wasn't easy," Cyrus tried to explain.

"So, now we're not twins. I don't get it. How are you taller than me?" Cyrus had easily grown a foot overnight.

Cyrus shook his head. "Not twins, no, but this

new face is an age-progression of you. So get a good look at how devastatingly handsome you'll be in ten years." Cyrus rubbed at his chin trying to make me laugh.

I didn't think it was funny, though. I could only stare and wonder what I'd done wrong to make Cyrus not want to be my twin brother anymore.

"And as for the height," Cyrus continued, "Mom added a few extra external hard drives so I can process data faster and store information without overloading my system. It should make things a lot easier for me, so I don't tire out so quickly. The drives were added to give me height, to help me look more like an adult human."

"So, what does this all mean? You don't want to be my brother anymore?" I'd been watching closely as he spoke and he still had a lot of the same movements he used to have, only he looked completely different on the outside and seemed a lot more energized.

Cyrus fiddled with the basketball on the table and then drew it closer to him. "We'll always be brothers, Shawn . . . "

I looked him in the eyes, "But—?"

"But, when I leave next week, I'm probably not coming back," he finished, frowning at his own words.

I felt a huge lump in my throat as I tried to understand what he was saying. "For a while? You're not coming back for a while, right?"

He shook his head slowly. "No, probably never."

My stomach clenched and I felt like he'd just punched me in the gut. I couldn't sit still. The emotions were swirling around and I didn't know what to do. So I stood up, grabbed my backpack, and walked away.

"Shawn, come on," Cyrus said, grabbing my arm when he caught up to me.

I shook him off and kept walking. I didn't have

anything to say to him. He was leaving. Just like that. No family discussion, no putting it to a vote.

"Shawn, please don't do this. I need to explain. Please let me explain," Cyrus called after me.

By this time I'd made it down the block, so I stopped and sat on the curb. "Fine, explain. This had better be good," I grumbled.

"Shawn, I'm a robot—"

I snorted, "Oh really? And all this time I thought you were a llama! Now it all makes sense."

"Come on, let me finish," Cyrus said.

I wiped tears of anger away from my face and nodded. "Fine."

"I'm a robot. I'm not human. I wasn't built to be human. I was built to help humans. When I joined your family, I learned so much about what it meant to be a human that I think I fooled myself into believing I was nearly human. But after learning about humans struggling to survive—which you taught me about, by the way—and creating the 3SNC, I just can't pretend to be a human kid anymore. I have the knowledge and capability to make life better for humans, and that's important to me. So, I'm a robot and I'm going to start acting like one," Cyrus finished and sounded like he took a deep breath.

I looked down at my shoelaces and traced the cracks in the pavement with my finger for a long time while I thought about what Cyrus had just said. He could create things that could save lives and he wanted to do it because he cared about humans. I knew it would be selfish to insist that he stay. "I'm really going to miss you," I whispered and let a few tears fall from my eyes.

Cyrus put an arm around my shoulder. "I'm going to miss you, too, Shawn. You're my best friend, brother, and you always will be."

We stood and started to walk home. I turned and

asked, "What did Dad say when he saw the new you?"

Cyrus laughed, "He told me that I looked like him as a young man and that he was going to miss me. And then he went into the kitchen and started cooking. I think there might be twelve vegetable side dishes for dinner when we get home."

I grinned. "Scooter is not going to be happy about that."

Cyrus shook his head. "No, he's not."

"What about Mom?" I asked wondering what would happen to her at work, since Cyrus was her project.

"The lab is assigning her to another artificial intelligence project. She was asked to head the AI department at Smith and Company Labs because of her success with me."

"So Dad will keep cooking and Mom will still be

busy at work. What about me? What happens to me?" I looked at my brother.

Cyrus smiled. "You'll be great. You are a smart, funny, and talented guy. And now you won't have a twin brother to compete with."

I laughed, "It was never much of a competition. You were always too perfect."

"You're right, it wasn't a competition, because you were always real. You had the advantage because you were human. And now you're a mature, awesome human with a long-distance, wonderful robot brother." Cyrus grinned.

I smirked and tapped the basketball Cyrus had carried with him from the park out of his hands and dribbled down the street a bit. The ball was heavier than the one we used at home.

"Where'd you get this ball?" I asked holding it up close to my face. I noticed some writing on the ball. I squinted, "Is that—"

"That was supposed to be a surprise. A going away present from me to you. See, when I was at a conference, I met the team and—"

"You met the team?!" I yelled, almost dropping the ball. "And you've been playing with an autographed ball? Wait! I've been dribbling a ball signed by the whole team?" I couldn't believe this was happening.

Cyrus shrugged. "It's just a ball."

"Just a ball?" I whispered, shaking my head. "Have you learned nothing about how sacred basketball is?"

Cyrus laughed, "Fine, I'll send you another one in a few weeks. I'll be back there for a symposium."

"So, you'll still be in touch? You're not going to abandon us completely?" I asked, feeling a little better.

"I could never abandon you. The Coles are my family. I just can't pretend to be human anymore. But we'll still call, text, email, video chat, and all that good stuff, deal?" Cyrus extended his hand to me.

And though I didn't want to lose my brother, I understood why I had to. I was prepared to share him with the world. So I reached out and we shook on it. "Okay, Cy. That's a deal."